This book belongs to:

. . . .

Also in the series:
A Cake for Miss Wand

THE FOREVER STREET FAIRIES: THE FAIRIES ARRIVE

by Hiawyn Oram and Mary Rees

British Library Cataloguing in Publication Data
A catalogue record of this book is available from
the British Library.

ISBN 0 340 84137 0

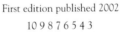

Text copyright © Hiawyn Oram 2002
Illustrations copyright © Mary Rees 2002

First edition published 2002
10 9 8 7 6 5 4 3

Published by Hodder Children's Books
a division of Hodder Headline Limited
338 Euston Road London NW1 3BH

Printed in Hong Kong

THE Forever Street Fairies

The Fairies Arrive

Written by

Hiawyn
Oram

Illustrated by

Mary
Rees

*Hodder
Children's
Books*

A division of Hodder Headline Limited

Contents

· · · · · · · · · ·

— Chapter One —

Baby Sighs, Fairies Born ... page 1

— Chapter Two —

All Here ... page 4

— Chapter Three —

Into The Woods ... page 8

— Chapter Four —

The Owl Points The Way ... page 14

— Chapter Five —

The Path Shows Itself ... page 20

— Chapter Six —

Miss Wand Opens The Gate ... page 27

— Chapter Seven —

Home Before Sunset ... page 32

To my mother
H. O.

To my good friend Ellen
M. R.

Chapter One
· · · · · · · · · · · · · · ·
Baby Sighs, Fairies Born

Nine babies were born
in St Mary's Hospital
that night.
They were snuggled
in their mothers' arms,
kissed,
cuddled
and fed.

1

Then came the sighs...
the first, soft, baby sighs
on which fairies are born.

The air above the cots stirred.
There was a fluttering
of almost invisible wings.
The mothers were too busy to notice.

The nurses and doctors
were too busy to notice.
And eight new fairies
and one pair of twin fairies
fluttered unseen...
out of the hospital
and into our world.

Chapter Two

· · · · · · · · · · · · · ·

All Here

They landed in a flower bed
just outside the hospital doors.
"Are we all here?" said Rainbow.
"I am," each fairy called.

"And we are," said Pea and Pod,
the Peaspod twins.

"Do we all have our magic?"
said Rainbow.

"I do," each fairy called.

"We do," said Pea and Pod,
waving their magic fishing rods
proudly.

"Then there's no time to lose,"
said Rainbow.
"We must set off
before the sun rises.
Or we'll be back
to where we were
before we got here."

Quickly, the new fairies
arranged themselves in a line
and linked hands.
Rainbow waved her wand
and a small rainbow appeared.
"That's the way," she called.
"So stay together and follow me!"

Chapter Three

Into The Woods

Fresh fairy dust twinkled
and like a string of fairy lights
the fairies rose up
behind Rainbow.
They left the town
before it was all awake...
and made good flying time
over the fields.

But soon the sun grew
burning hot.
They could no longer see
the rainbow...
and the twins began
to wilt and fade.

"We must get them
into the shade!" called Speedwell.
"Down there...
into those woods!"

Holding the twins,
the fairies
swooped down
after Speedwell...
and landed
on a cushion of moss
and mushrooms.

Speedwell clicked her magic
stopwatch.
"This'll stop time for a bit
so they won't fade any further.
But we'll need dew to revive them!"
"I'll go for it!" cried Fingers.
"My fingers will feel out anything!"

Moments later
she returned with an acorn cup
filled with the last dewdrops
of the day.
Speedwell splashed it
over the twins.
Almost at once, they revived,
chuckling and hugging each
other.

This made them all laugh.
"What a happy band we're going
to be!" said Bristle. "When
we get to where we're going."
"If we ever do," said Nogo.
"Which we won't,"
said Mr Snip Snap. "Unless
we find the path soon."

Chapter Four

The Owl Points The Way

Rainbow shifted her handbag.

"The path! Of course!

There always is a path!"

The fairies looked around.

They saw
trees and grass,
shafts of
sunlight,
brambles and
wild flowers
but not a sign
of a path.
"I know!" cried
Bristle. "I'll sweep us a path with
my magic brush!"
Busily, he got to work
and swept a path
that led all by itself
straight to the tallest pine tree.

"But where's the door?"
said Speedwell. "There always
is a door."
"It might be higher up," said Elfie,
swirling his magic flying cloak.
"I'll take a look."
Halfway up
Elfie found a door
set in the trunk of the tree.

There was no knocker
so he pushed and it opened.
"TWHOOOOO enters
without knocking?"
A large owl put out a claw
and trapped Elfie under it.

"Uh... only me, Elfie the Elf,"
stammered Elfie,
shaking like a leaf.
"Looking for the door
at the end of the path.
To get to where we're going
before the sun sets.

Or we'll be back to where we were,

before we got here…"

"Then why bother me?"

The owl opened his claw,

closed his eyes and yawned.

"Ask a squirrel to show you

the way."

Chapter Five
The Path Shows Itself

"Wrong door," Elfie panted when
he got back to the others.
"But I did find out something!
We need a squirrel
to show us the way!"
Rainbow took her wand
from her handbag.
"I'll try for one," she said,
and threw another small
but perfect rainbow.

"No go," chuckled Nogo.
"There's a PAIL at the end
of it, not a squirrel!"
"There may be a squirrel
IN the pail," said Luckyday.
They all fluttered over
to the pail.

"No go!" said Nogo.

"No squirrel."

"Not yet," said Elfie.

"But what's that?"

A small squirrel had
appeared on a branch
above the pail.

With one big leap
she was in the pail
and stuffing herself
with nuts.

"Magic!" she said
with her mouth full.
"Never tasted such magic nuts!
And as we say in these woods,
one magic turn
deserves another...

23

So what can I do for you?"

"Show us the path," said Elfie.

"To where we're going,"

said Fingers, "before the sun sets."

"Or we'll be back to where we

were before we got here,"

said Rainbow.

"Ah, THAT path,"

said the squirrel.

"We call it Forever Street
because it begins anywhere
and probably goes on forever.
Anyone can see it if they look.
So look."
The squirrel grabbed the last nut,
waved her tail
and scampered off.

And as the fairies watched
they saw what they hadn't seen
before...
There WAS a path
through the woods.
It was appearing, as if by magic,
behind the squirrel,
wherever she ran.

26

Chapter Six

Miss Wand Opens The Gate

Miss Wand had been waiting

for fairies.

She knew they existed.

She always had.

She had just finished feeding

the hedgehogs

who lived in the woods

at the bottom of her garden...

27

when something caught her eye.
A tiny apricot dress
in the long grass.

A blue cap in the clover.
A fluttering of wings...
The swish of a red flying cloak.

"Oh Cyclone!"

She picked up her cat.

"Could it be? I believe it is!"

She ran inside.

She shut Cyclone

in her kitchen.

From the old dolls' house
in her second-hand toy shop
she took beds, a table,
six chairs.
And a set of golden plates,
cups and saucers.

Back in her garden,
she placed them
in the long grass,
as if they'd fallen there
by themselves.
Then she quietly opened the gate
from the garden into the woods.

Chapter Seven

· · · · · · · · · · · · · · · ·

Home Before Sunset

As soon as the fairies were on
the Forever Street path,
they knew it was their path.
"And do look," said Speedwell
pointing ahead.
"There's the door."

They fluttered up to the gate
Miss Wand had just opened.
And one by one they tripped
through it...
into Miss Wand's back garden.

At once they saw it was just right
for fairy life.
The grass was long.
The flowers and herbs grew
as they liked.
The apple trees were old.
Bees buzzed.

Butterflies fluttered.
A big brown
butterfly flew up.
"She's left something
for you," he said.
"Who has?"
said Rainbow.
"The One Who Treads Softly.
The One Who Opened the Gate.
Come and I'll show you."

The butterfly led the fairies
to the dolls' house furniture.
They stared in wonder.
"It's as if we were expected!"
cried Elfie.
"You were!" said the butterfly.

"Then we must have arrived,"
said Speedwell, "where
we set out for."
"And where we are going,"
said Rainbow.

37

"And I'm STARVING!"
said Mr Snip Snap.
"Is there anything to eat
round here?"
"Everything," said the butterfly.
He showed them the nectar
in the honeysuckle...
and the berries on the bushes.

Fingers filled the golden cups
with evening dew.
Speedwell laid the table.

Rainbow used her wand to
change the colour of her dress...
and they sat down to
their first supper together.
There were not enough
cups, saucers, plates or chairs
to go round
but it did not matter.

The sun had not set
and the new fairies
of Forever Street were home.
And across the fields and woods
it was as if the babies
who had breathed them knew.
They stirred in their cots
and then,
like the fairies
in Miss Wand's garden,
they smiled secretly...
and slept.